THE CHINESE EMPEROR'S NEW CLOTHES

By Ying Chang Compestine
Illustrated by David Roberts

Abrams Books for Young Readers, New York

By now, you have probably heard the old folktale about the emperor's new clothes. Two sly tailors fool a vain emperor into believing he is wearing magical clothes, when in fact he is parading through town buck naked. The truth is that the story took place here in China, and without any tricky tailors.

Here is the real story.

When Ming Da was nine, he became the emperor of China. His ministers thought the boy emperor was too young to rule and took advantage of him. They stole silks to make themselves fine clothes. They stole rice from the emperor's warehouses and sold it to dishonest merchants. And they robbed the royal treasury of gold and precious stones.

They left the boy emperor with no cloth to dress the poor, no food to feed the hungry, and no money to run his kingdom. Ming Da knew that if he fired the corrupt ministers, they would rebel against him.

Day and night, the boy emperor searched for a way to save his kingdom, but he couldn't think of anything. Until . . .

. . . a month before Chinese New Year. Traditionally, people dress in new clothes on New Year's Day so evil spirits won't recognize them. When Ming Da's loyal tailors came with the design for his new clothes, the boy emperor was gazing out the window at the children begging on the streets.

"You will look magnificent in the parade!" the old tailor said, holding the cloth higher.

Ming Da glanced at the dragon stitched above fluffy clouds. He wished he could dress the street children just as finely.

"Do you like it?" asked the young tailor.

"Very nice!" said Ming Da, staring at the crow, monkey, and rat fleeing from the dragon.

Suddenly, he had an idea. "My ministers are stealing from me. Will you help me outwit them?"

"Of course!" said his tailors.

So Ming Da told them his plan.

The next day, Ming Da summoned his ministers.

"I want to show you the magical new clothes these fine tailors made for me," he said.

"Magical?" asked the Agriculture Minister skeptically.

"Yes! Honest people will see their true splendor, while the dishonest will see only burlap sacks," said the young tailor.

"Please show us!" said the plump War Minister.

"Certainly!" Ming Da hopped off his throne and stepped behind a screen. The tailors helped him put on an old rice sack painted with ink and vegetable juices.

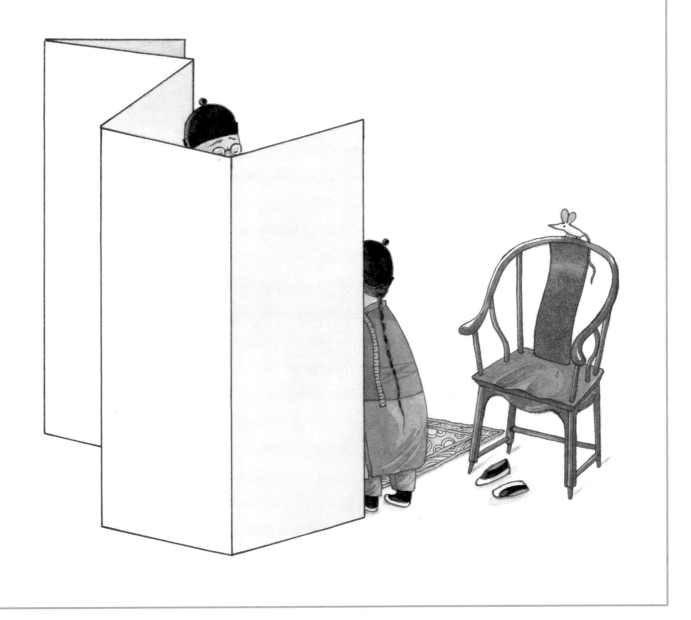

When Ming Da stepped out, the ministers stared at the boy emperor, mouths agape.

"Most excellent, don't you think?" Ming Da spread his arms wide. "Feel the sleeves!" He shook his arms.

The Trade Minister broke into a cold sweat. He stroked the rough sack. "Um, it's softer than the finest silk!"

"Th-th-the dra-dragons' eyes are so alive!" stuttered the War Minister.

"We used the finest black pearls from the South China Sea," said the young tailor.

The ministers exclaimed their approval, each louder than the last.

"Unbelievable!"

"Astonishing!"

"Magnificent!"

"These tailors are at your service. Who wants magical new clothes?" asked the young emperor.

The ministers quickly raised their hands.

"Excellent! Tailors, get to work!" ordered Ming Da.

So the tailors set up cutting tables, coffers, and trunks behind a large screen. They "worked" day and night!

The news about the magical clothes spread like fire in a dry field. The citizens looked forward to seeing the lavish new robes at the New Year's Day parade, except the dishonest merchants.

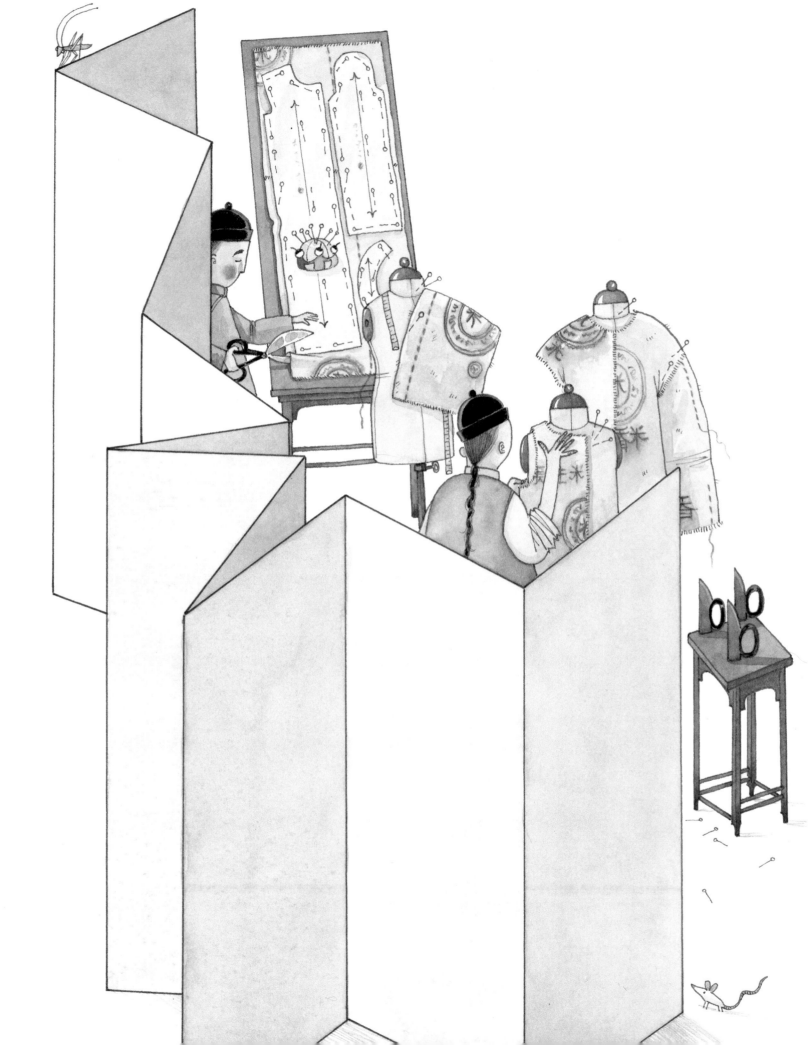

Soon came the fitting for the ministers.

Ming Da skipped his daily visit to the orphanage and hid behind a screen to watch.

When the Trade Minister entered, the young tailor held up a rice sack. "See how the rubies and pearls in the crow's eyes and beak sparkle in the light?"

Face pale, the minister glared at the tailor. "Why is there only one crow?" he demanded.

"We ran out of jewels," said the young tailor.

"I will supply all the jewels you need. Just make mine more splendid than the others!" He stormed out without trying on his new clothes.

When the War Minister entered, the young tailor held up a rice sack.

"Don't you love the extravagant details of the clever monkey?"

The minister squinted his eyes at the drawing of a sly monkey stealing gold. "It is unbelievable! Let me try it on!"

The tailors helped him into his robe and tightly wrapped a straw rope around his chubby waist.

"How does it fit?" asked the young tailor.

"Can you make it bigger?" The minister gasped for air and waved his arms about.

"Yes, but we ran out of silk," said the young tailor.

"I will pay with the purest gold. Just make mine more splendid than the others," he ordered.

When the Agriculture Minister entered, the old tailor was busily trimming the bottom of a rice sack with scissors.

The minister looked at it from all angles. Beads of sweat rolled down his face.

"See how the rat's shiny eyes look alive?"

"Yes, it's astonishing!" The minister stared at the drawing of a long-whiskered rat stealing rice. The tailors helped the minister into his robe.

"How does it fit?" asked the young tailor.

The minister looked down at his bare legs. "Can you make it longer?" He rubbed his knobby knees.

"We ran out of silk," said the young tailor.

"I will pay you with the best rice that you can trade. Just make mine more splendid than the others," he ordered.

In the days that followed, the ministers delivered baskets of precious gems, gold, and rice to the tailors.

With the jewels and gold, Ming Da bought cloth to dress the poor. With the rice, the emperor fed them.

Soon came the morning of the New Year's Day parade. When Ming Da entered the hall in his new clothes, the ministers were loudly praising one another.

"Unbelievable!" exclaimed the Trade Minister.

"Astonishing!" cried the War Minister.

"Magnificent!" shouted the Agriculture Minister.

"You all look splendid! Let the parade begin!" declared the boy emperor.

Lion dancers led the way. Firecrackers popped and exploded, martial artists punched and kicked, and acrobats jumped and tumbled.

At last, the ministers came marching behind Ming Da, proudly showing off their new robes. The street fell silent, and whispers spread throughout the crowd.

"Um, spectacular!" said one of the dishonest merchants.

"Beautiful fabric!" said another.

"Lovely design!" said a third.

"Can you not see? They're wearing rice sacks!" shrieked a boy. The crowd roared with laughter.

Ming Da smiled as the children sang and pointed. "Itchy sacks! Itchy sacks!"

"You *are* wearing rice sacks!" exclaimed the War Minister to the other two.

"So are *you*!" cried the Trade Minster.

"We have been tricked!" shouted the Agriculture Minister.

The ministers fled China. Ming Da replaced them with honest counselors and ruled for many years. His people were happy, well fed, and very well dressed.

Now that's the real story! The emperor marched through the town to save his country. I don't know how people ended up with that old folktale about two sly tailors fooling a vain emperor.

AUTHOR'S NOTE

In Ancient China, the emperor often appointed his favorite son to succeed him to the throne, regardless of age. When Pu Yi, the last emperor of China, came to power in 1908, he was less than three years old!

The Chinese use a lunar calendar based on the phases of the moon. Chinese New Year usually occurs between mid-January and early February. The most important part of the celebration is a parade, which is often led by officials, followed by dancing dragons, firecrackers, acrobatic performances, and lion dancers.

According to Chinese tradition, on New Year's Day it is important that everyone dresses in new clothes. That way they can have a fresh start, and evil spirits won't recognize them.

I grew up during the Chinese Cultural Revolution (1966–1976). Like the street children in this story, we were deprived of food and clothes along with many other things. For example, Western fairy tales, folktales, and novels were banned and burned. But that didn't stop my family and me from reading: My brothers and I read every work of literature that came into our hands, and my parents read banned medical journals.

Whenever I was lucky enough to get my hands on one of the *forbidden* books, I had to read it in a hurry, late at night, so I could pass it on to friends who were anxiously awaiting their turn. If caught, we could face public humiliation and even risked having our families sent to a labor camp.

Despite the danger, the hunger for literature was so intense that we were willing to risk it. Like the boy emperor, I always searched for ways to outsmart the officials. I would hide the banned books between newspapers or wrap them in lotus leaves. My most daring trick was disguising the book with the jacket of a government propaganda book.

Due to the lack of books and other entertainment, my friends and I would pass the time by reciting stories from the illegal books we had read. On my eighth Chinese New Year's Eve, a friend lent me a dog-eared translation of the forbidden *The Emperor's New Clothes* by Hans Christian Andersen. I stayed up all night, reading it over and over. I traced my fingers over the beautiful illustrations. I laughed out loud at the naked emperor marching through town.

When it was my turn to recite a story, I added my own twist to *The Emperor's New Clothes*, and rewarded myself and my friends with new clothes and food for the upcoming New Year. That experience eventually led to this retelling.

Ying in China during the Cultural Revolution

MAKE YOUR OWN CHINESE NEW YEAR PARADE ROBE

With the help of an adult, you can make your own robe by following the steps below and hold your own Chinese New Year parade!

You will need:

Scissors

White pillowcase or old T-shirt

Some dried beans, white or black rice, buttons, plastic beads, or colorful dried pasta

Ribbons

Fabric markers

Fabric paint

Craft glue

Cardboard or a brown paper bag

Instructions:

1. Have an adult help you cut holes in the pillowcase for your head and arms. Or use a T-shirt.

2. Place a piece of cardboard or a brown paper bag inside the pillowcase to prevent ink and glue from seeping through to the other side.

3. Pick a design you like and, with a fabric marker, trace it onto the front and back of the pillowcase.

4. Decorate your robe by gluing on beans, rice, buttons, plastic beads, dried pasta, and ribbons.

5. Lay the robe out to dry overnight. Then decorate the other side.

6. Hold your own Chinese New Year parade!

For Lucy Williams

—D. R.

To Vinson, Ming Da,
my little emperor who's all grown up

—Y. C. C.

Years ago I worked in fashion design and lived in Hong Kong.
When I read this manuscript, I was intrigued by the idea of
bringing my love of fashion to a world of silk robes and burlap
bags. I wish to thank Ying for her suggestions and the reference
materials she provided. The palace, interiors, and clothes are
not meant to be an exact replica of those in China. I have tweaked
the setting a bit, just as Ying has done with the story. This is the
China of a little emperor who wishes to save his kingdom.

—David Roberts

The illustrations in this book were made with watercolors, pen, and ink on
Arches paper. For some pieces, pencil and graph paper were also employed.

Cataloging-in-Publication Data has been applied for and may be obtained
from the Library of Congress.

Library of Congress Control Number 2016036496
ISBN 978-1-4197-2542-5

Text copyright © 2017 Ying Compestine
Illustrations copyright © 2017 David Roberts
Book design by Chad W. Beckerman and Tree Abraham

Printed and bound in U.S.A.
10 9 8 7 6 5 4 3 2 1

Abrams Books for Young Readers are available at special discounts when
purchased in quantity for premiums and promotions as well as fundraising
or educational use. Special editions can also be created to specification.
For details, contact specialsales@abramsbooks.com or the address below.

ABRAMS The Art of Books
115 West 18th Street, New York, NY 10011
abramsbooks.com